# A Snowy Day in BUGLAND!

by David A. Carter

Ready-to-Read

Simon Spotlight
New York   London   Toronto   Sydney   New Delhi

SIMON SPOTLIGHT
An imprint of Simon & Schuster Children's Publishing Division
1230 Avenue of the Americas, New York, New York 10020
SIMON SPOTLIGHT, READY-TO-READ, and colophon are registered trademarks of Simon & Schuster, Inc.
For information about special discounts for bulk purchases, please contact Simon & Schuster Special Sales
at 1-866-506-1949 or business@simonandschuster.com.
Manufactured in the United States of America 0812 LAK
First Edition
10 9 8 7 6 5 4 3 2 1
Library of Congress Cataloging-in-Publication Data
Carter, David A.
A snowy day in Bugland / by David A. Carter. — 1st ed.
p. cm. — (Ready-to-read)
Summary: Busy Bug helps Bitsy Bee enjoy her first snow day in Bugland.
ISBN 978-1-4424-3895-8 (hardcover)
ISBN 978-1-4424-3894-1 (pbk.)
ISBN 978-1-4424-3896-5 (eBook)
[etc.]
[1. Stories in rhyme. 2. Bees—Fiction. 3. Insects—Fiction. 4. Snow—Fiction.] I. Title.
PZ8.3.C244Sno 2012 [E]—dc23 2011031809

Brr!
Snow has come to
Bugland!

A family of Snowflake Bugs
flutter to the ground.

The happy Ice-Skating Bug
twirls round and round.

The Thermometer Bug is shivering in the chilly breeze.

The Icicle Bugs are hanging out, enjoying the big freeze.

Inside the cozy pumpkin
house, Bitsy Bee opens
her eyes wide.

Beyond the frosty
window, the world is
bright and white
outside.

One little bug is ready for
her very first snow day!

Bitsy can hardly wait to
go outside and play!

Bitsy Bee is so excited.
She runs across the
floor.

Mama Bug stops Bitsy Bee.
She points at the closet
door.

"The air is cold today," says Mama Bug. "Be sure to bundle up tight!"

The Coat and Mitten Bugs
keep Bitsy warm.
Bitsy feels just right.

*Whoosh! Swoosh! Crunch!*
Busy Bug comes sledding by.

Busy Bug asks Bitsy if she would like to try.

Up and over snow hills,
these friends glide and dip.

Hang on tight, you
buggy friends!
Be careful not to slip!

Wild and crazy Snowball Bugs
fly from behind the
snow pile.

A snowball lands on Busy's head. Bitsy starts to smile.

It is almost time for this snow day to come to an end.

So, Bitsy and Busy build a
Snowman Bug to be their
winter friend.

Hooray for snow in Bugland!